MY ADVENTURES

WITH

Disney's

Snow White
and the Seven Dwarfs

This book was especially written for
Chloe Gomola
With love from
Grammy and Pappy

Adapted by Wendy Elks

ISBN 1 875676 15 5

One day Chloe and her friends were playing in a large, rambling garden. In an overgrown corner, Chloe found a funny little wooden gate set in an archway, with a tangled rose bush growing over it. Through the gate she could see a beautiful meadow.

There was a forest in the distance, and far away, surrounded by mist, she saw the faint outline of a large castle. Chloe decided to go through the gate and look around, just for a moment or two.

As soon as Chloe walked into the meadow she felt different. There seemed to be magic in the air. Chloe wandered further than she meant to. She couldn't stop exploring — it was such a beautiful place!

But when she turned around to go back, Chloe discovered that she was lost.

Chloe walked on and on, but the forest was deep and thick. She had no idea where the meadow with the little gate was. She was tired, so she sat down to rest. Suddenly she noticed that she was surrounded by forest animals.

They were looking at her kindly, as if they knew she was lost, too. 'You know I'm a stranger here, don't you?' Chloe said to them. 'I wish I knew how to get home again.'

A lovely fawn walked off a little way and stopped to look back at Chloe. Chloe was sure that the fawn wanted her to follow. Soon she was running along behind a whole group of animals and birds.

The animals led her deep into the forest, to a beautiful girl who was collecting flowers. The girl laughed as the animals surrounded her joyfully. She sat on the ground and put her arms around as many of them as she could.

'Hello,' said the girl, smiling at Chloe. 'I'm Snow White.'

'Hello, Snow White,' said Chloe. 'My name is Chloe Gomola, and I'm lost. I live at 737 7th Street, Pitcairn. Do you know how I can get back there?'

Snow White shook her head. 'No, I'm afraid I don't. I live here in the forest. But come with me.'

As they walked, Snow White told Chloe about the wicked Queen who lived in the castle. Snow White had lived there too, once upon a time. But the Queen hated Snow White, because Snow White was more beautiful than she was.

She had tried to destroy Snow White but the huntsman who had been sent to kill her felt sorry for her and set her free in the forest. 'I was lost and lonely, too,' said Snow White. 'But now I live with the Seven Dwarfs. We look after each other. They mine gold in the mountains, and I look after their house for them. We'll go and see them now. Perhaps they will know how to get to Pitcairn.'

They came to a dear little cottage deep in the forest. The Seven Dwarfs were away at work. Chloe helped Snow White with her chores. They washed the floors together, and then went upstairs to make the beds.

While Snow White made a big pot of soup for dinner, she told Chloe all about the handsome prince who lived in another kingdom far away.

'One day he'll find me, and take me away forever,' said Snow White. 'Then I won't have to worry about the wicked Queen any more. But I had to run away from the castle, and now he doesn't know where to find me.'

As the sun was setting that evening, Chloe heard far-off singing and whistling. 'What's that?' she asked Snow White.

'It's the Dwarfs!' cried Snow White. 'Let's go and meet them!'

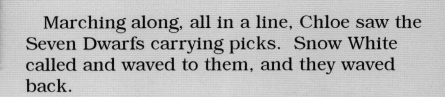

Marching along, all in a line, Chloe saw the Seven Dwarfs carrying picks. Snow White called and waved to them, and they waved back.

'This is Chloe Gomola,' Snow White told them as they marched up. 'She was lost in the forest, and she doesn't know how to get home.'

The Dwarfs washed their hands and faces and they all sat down to dinner. None of them knew where Pitcairn was, or the meadow with the gate that Chloe had come through.

'There are many gates into this land, and many meadows,' said Doc. 'It's too dark to go searching now, but we'll come home early tomorrow, and help you look then.'

'Thank you,' said Chloe. 'That's very kind of you. I know how much my family and my friends will be worrying about me.'

'I have an idea that might cheer Chloe up, and take her mind off missing her family!' said Doc. 'Let's have a party!'

Everyone thought that was a wonderful idea. The Dwarfs sang songs together and played musical instruments, and Snow White danced and sang beautifully. Doc handed Chloe a drum so she could join in.

While they were singing and dancing that night in the cottage in the forest, the Queen was busy in the dungeon of her castle. She was hard at work in her secret chamber making spells because her Magic Mirror had told her that Snow White was still alive, and tomorrow the Queen was planning to pay the girl a visit!

The wicked Queen mixed up a poisonous potion and dipped a beautiful red apple into it. Then she transformed herself into an ugly old woman.

'One bite of this apple,' hissed the Queen, 'and Snow White will fall down into a deathly sleep. Only love's first kiss will revive her. But the Dwarfs will think she's dead!' The Queen cackled and rubbed her bony hands together in delight!

When Chloe woke up the next morning, the Dwarfs had already gone to work. Snow White was sweeping the floor.

'I'd love some help,' said Snow White. 'Would you go out into the forest and collect some firewood, Chloe? If I finish my chores early, I can come with you and the Dwarfs to find the gate that will lead you back home.'

So Chloe went out to collect firewood. On her way back, she saw an old woman in a black cloak approaching the cottage.

Chloe had a bad feeling. There was something strange about the old woman. Chloe followed her to the cottage, keeping out of sight. She didn't want the old woman to see her.

She saw the black-cloaked figure knock at the door of the cottage. She was holding a small basket. Snow White opened the door and invited the woman in. Chloe crept up to the window and peered inside. The old woman had taken a shiny red apple out of her basket.

'Eat this magic apple,' said the woman. 'And your deepest wish will come true.'

'Oh, really?' said Snow White happily. I'll wish for my prince to find me!' Snow White took a bite of the apple, and fell to the floor.

With a horrible cackling laugh, the old woman quickly left the cottage. When Chloe was sure the woman had gone she raced inside.

'Oh poor Snow White!' cried Chloe. 'Snow White, can you hear me?'

Snow White looked pale and ill, and Chloe couldn't wake her.

'Oh, no! What shall I do?' thought Chloe to herself. 'I wish my friends were here to help me.'

With the help of four little birds, Chloe put Snow White to bed. She then went outside to find the Dwarfs — Doc might know how to make Snow White better! Chloe had no idea where the Dwarfs might be, but then she saw the fawn grazing nearby.

'Fawn, you must go and find the Dwarfs! I can't wake Snow White.'

The fawn seemed to understand and she ran off towards the mountains. Chloe went back inside to care for Snow White, but there was really nothing she could do. At last she saw the Dwarfs coming towards the cottage. She ran out to meet them.

'Snow White is sick!' she cried. 'I think she might have been poisoned!'

'What happened?' asked Doc.

Chloe told them about the old woman with the apple.

'That was the Queen in disguise,' said Doc. 'She wants to get Snow White!' The Dwarfs were terribly upset.

'Snow White is dead,' said Doc sadly, when they came out of her room. All of the Dwarfs were crying.

'Let's find the Queen, before she goes back to the castle!' yelled Grumpy. 'We won't let her get away with it!'

They all ran outside. Chloe and the Dwarfs leapt onto the fawns. Chloe hung on tightly as it scampered after the others towards the castle.

Chloe was scared of the wicked Queen, but she felt safe surrounded by the Dwarfs. They chased the Queen up a steep cliff. She slipped and fell from sight. The wicked Queen was gone.

They all went back to the cottage and carried Snow White out into the forest. They laid her gently on a bench and surrounded her with flowers.

Just then Chloe saw a man on a white horse in the distance.

The man on the white horse came towards them.

When he saw Snow White, he bent over her
sadly. Then he touched his lips to hers.
Snow White opened her eyes. She wasn't dead
after all! She cried out happily and threw her
arms around the Prince's neck.

Doc told the prince what had happened. The prince looked at Chloe. 'If you hadn't been with Snow White she might have died,' he said. 'When is your birthday?'

'On September 4th' answered Chloe.

The prince took a small sack from his pocket and chose a beautiful jewel. 'The sapphire is your birthstone. Please take it to remember us by.'

'Do you know of a wooden gate in a meadow?' asked Chloe. 'I need to find it, so I can go home to Pitcairn.'

The prince knew of the meadow, and took Chloe to the gate. The prince and Snow White waved goodbye and rode off to his kingdom where they lived happily ever after.